ATHENEUM BOOKS FOR YOUNG READERS · An imprint of Simon & Schuster Children's Publishing Division · 1230 Avenue of the Americas, New York, New York 10020 · Copyright © 2011 by Andy Runton · All rights reserved, including the right of reproduction in whole or in part in any form. · OWLY is a trademark of Andy Runton · ATHENEUM BOOKS FOR YOUNG READERS is a registered trademark of Simon & Schuster, Inc. · For information about special discounts for bulk purchases, please contact Simon & Schuster Special Sales at 1-866-506-1949 or business@simonandschuster.com. · The Simon & Schuster Speakers Bureau can bring authors to your live event. For more information or to book an event, contact the Simon & Schuster Speakers Bureau at 1-866-248-3049 or visit our website at www.simonspeakers.com. · Book design by Sonia Chaghatzbanian and Michael McCartney · The illustrations for this book are drawn and inked by hand and painted using digital pastels. · Manufactured in China · 1210 SCP · First Edition · 10 9 8 7 6 5 4 3 2 1 · Library of Congress Cataloging-in-Publication Data · Runton, Andy. · Owly and Wormy, friends all aflutter! / Andy Runton. — 1st ed. · Summary: Good friends Owly and Wormy are disappointed when their new plant attracts fat, green buglike things, instead of butterflies, until a metamorphosis occurs. · ISBN 978-1-4169-5774-4 [1. Owls—Fiction. 2. Worms—Fiction. 3. Butterflies—Fiction 4. Metamorphosis—Fiction. 5. Stories without words.] I. Title. · PZ7.R8882970w 2011 · [E]—dc22 · 2010006123

Owly & Wormy
FRIENDS ALL AFLUTTER!

ANDY RUNTON

ATHENEUM BOOKS FOR YOUNG READERS / NEW YORK · LONDON · TORONTO · SYDNEY